Rag, Tag and Bobtail
and other Stories

By the same author

Enid Blyton

Rag, Tag and Bobtail
and other stories

Illustrated by Eileen A. Soper

DRAGON
GRAFTON BOOKS
A Division of the Collins Publishing Group

LONDON GLASGOW
TORONTO SYDNEY AUCKLAND

Dragon
Grafton Books
A Division of the Collins Publishing Group
8 Grafton Street, London W1X 3LA

Published by Dragon Books 1975
Reprinted 1977, 1979, 1981, 1986

First published in Great Britain by Macmillan & Co Ltd
under the title *The Three Naughty Children and
Other Stories* 1950

Copyright © Darrell Waters Ltd 1950

ISBN 0-583-30220-3

Printed and bound in Great Britain by
Collins, Glasgow

Set in Monotype Baskerville

Contents

Rag, Tag and Bobtail

Rag, Tag and Bobtail were three small pixies, all as mischievous as could be. They lived together in Windy Cottage and worked for old Lady Grumble, the wise woman on the hill.

Rag scrubbed the floors, Tag swept and Bobtail dusted. For this work Lady Grumble paid them sixpence a day each, which didn't buy them anything very grand to eat or to wear. But they were so quarrelsome that nobody else would give them work, and old Lady Grumble didn't mind how they quarrelled, for she was deaf and couldn't hear.

Rag and the others were half afraid of the wise woman, for she knew a great deal of magic. She knew how to make spells, and how to grant wishes, she knew how to turn people into frogs and how to change a beetle into a prince. She really was very clever indeed.

When she first had the three pixies to work for her she warned them on no account to touch any of her magic bottles or boxes.

'You don't know what may happen if you begin to meddle with magic you know nothing about,' she said. 'So keep your little fingers away from my magic cupboard, Rag, Tag and Bobtail.'

For a long time they did – and then one day Rag found a little yellow box on the floor.

'Look!' he cried, pointing with his scrubbing brush. 'There's a tiny yellow box. It must have fallen out of Lady Grumble's magic cupboard. One of you pick it up and look inside to see what there is in it.'

'Look inside it yourself!' cried Tag. 'Coward!'

'I'm *not* a coward!' cried Rag, and he boldly picked up the box. 'Ho, coward am I, Tag? Well, I've picked it up – and now *you* can open the box!'

And with that the rude pixie threw the box straight into Tag's surprised face. The box burst open and out fell many tiny purple pills.

The pixies stared at them in astonishment, for they knew quite well what they were! They were wishing-pills! Whoever swallowed one of those purple pills and wished would have his wish come true.

'I say!' said Bobtail, looking down at the pills. 'Shall we keep them and eat them?'

'No,' said Rag. 'Lady Grumble would find out and punish us.'

'We could wish her away to the moon!' cried Tag.

'No, let's go and tell her we found the box of wishing-pills and ask her to let us have one each,' said Tag. 'She will think we are very honest pixies, then, and will perhaps reward us for being good.'

So Tag picked up the pills, put them back into the yellow box, and then all three of the pixies went to tell Lady Grumble. She was lying down in the back room of her cottage, thinking out a wonderful moonlight spell. They had to shout at her to make her hear what they had to say.

When she understood that they had found the pills and were bringing them to her, she seemed pleased. But she shook her head when they asked her if she would let them have a pill each.

'Wishes are only for sweet-natured people,' she said. 'Bad-tempered and quarrelsome creatures like you should never be allowed to have wishes. You only do harm.'

'Oh, please, please let us have a wish each,' said Rag. 'We won't quarrel, we won't be bad-tempered, we'll be good and kind. Really and truly.'

He had to shout it all over again before Lady Grumble heard what he said. She looked at him and shook her head doubtfully.

'Well, well,' she said, opening the box of

pills. 'I'll do as you say – but mind, pixies, if
you are *not* kind and loving to one another,
you will find that the wishes do you harm
instead of good. So be careful!'

Joyfully the pixies popped a pill into their
mouths and thanked Lady Grumble. Then
they ran to the kitchen to talk about their
good fortune.

'Think of it!' said Rag, jumping up and
down in delight. 'A wish for each of us! What
shall we wish? Who will wish first?'

'Shall we wish to be very rich indeed?' said
Tag.

'Or shall we wish never to work any more,'
shouted Bobtail.

'What about wishing for a palace bigger than the King's?' said Rag. 'That *would* be exciting!'

'And a hundred servants!' cried Tag.

'And chocolate pudding and ice-cream for dinner every day!' said Bobtail, smacking his lips in delight. 'Ooh! How I wish we could have a great big ice-cream each now! I'm so hot and . . .'

He stopped – for before him on the table appeared three very large ice-creams, one strawberry, one vanilla and one chocolate!

Rag, Tag and Bobtail stared at them in the greatest dismay – and then Rag turned on Bobtail in rage.

'You silly, stupid, foolish, ridiculous pixie!' he cried, angrily. 'Look what you've wasted your wish on! Just look!'

'Yes, look!' shouted Tag. 'Three silly ice-creams, when we could have had sacks and sacks of gold! Oh, you booby!'

'Booby yourself!' cried Bobtail, in a rage too. 'I didn't think what I was saying, that's all! I just said it and they came, those three ice-creams!'

'Well you've wasted your wish nicely,' said Rag. 'Tag and I are not going to be so silly.

We are going to wish for a big palace and lots of servants.'

'No, I'm not,' said Tag. 'I've thought of something else I'd rather have. I want a nice white horse to ride on. I've always wanted a white horse.'

'White horse!' cried Rag. 'You silly

creature! Fancy wanting a white horse when you could have all the stables in the world! Why not wish for a *hundred* white horses if you want such a silly thing!'

'It's *not* a silly thing to want!' said Tag, fiercely. 'Mind what you're saying, Rag. And look out for those ice-creams, you silly pixie! You've knocked mine on to the floor! I shall have *yours*!'

He was just going to pick up Rag's ice-cream and eat it when that bad-tempered little pixie picked it up himself and threw it at the astonished Tag.

'There!' cried Rag, angrily. 'Have it if you like – and may it drip all down your neck till it makes you cough and sneeze without stopping!'

The ice-cream splashed into Tag's face, and began to drip down his neck. Tag tried to wipe it away but it wouldn't be wiped. It stuck there, dripping, dripping, dripping! The wish had come true!

'Oh, Rag, you wished a wish!' said Bobtail in horror. 'What a horrid wish! Poor Tag! He'll have ice-cream dripping down his neck for ever, and he'll cough and sneeze all day long!'

Sure enough Tag soon began to cough and sneeze without stopping, for the ice-cream was giving him a dreadful cold. Whatever was he to do?

'A-tishoo, a-tish-oo!' sneezed Tag, trying to find his handkerchief. 'Oh, you horrid thing, Rag! Look what you've done! Go and fetch Lady Grumble and ask her to take the nasty ice-cream away!'

So Rag fetched Lady Grumble and when she came and saw poor Tag with ice-cream running down his neck and heard him sneezing and coughing twenty times a minute, she *was* surprised.

'Please stop the ice-cream dripping down Tag's neck,' begged Rag, nearly crying.

'But how did it get there?' asked Lady Grumble in great surprise.

'I wasted a wish and wished for ice-creams each,' said Bobtail, hanging his head.

'And I quarrelled with Tag and used my wish in wishing that his ice-cream should drip down his neck and make him cough and sneeze,' said Rag, very red indeed. 'And it's come true, though I didn't mean to wish it. Please, please, Lady Grumble, take away the spell.'

'But what about the third wish?' asked Lady Grumble. 'Hasn't Tag wished his wish yet?'

'Not yet,' said Rag.

'Well, why doesn't he use it to get rid of the ice-cream and to stop it dripping down his neck?' asked the wise woman.

'What, waste my wish in wishing a thing like that!' cried Tag, crossly. 'Not I! I'm keeping my wish for something grand. I'll be a rich man when Rag and Bobtail are poor! I'll show them what I can do with *my* wish! I'll punish Rag for doing this to me! A-tishoo! A-tishoo!'

'You are all three horrid, quarrelsome, unkind and selfish pixies!' said Lady Grumble, in disgust. 'I certainly shan't do anything to help you, Tag. If you want to get rid of that ice-cream, you can wish it away. But if you'd rather have it dripping down your neck all your life long, and be a rich man, well, you can choose!'

Tag stared at the wise woman in dismay.

'A-tishoo!' he said. 'Lady Grumble! Do, I beg of you, take away this spell and let me use my wish as I like! A-tishoo!'

But Lady Grumble seemed to become deaf again all of a sudden, and walked out of the room, laughing to herself. The three pixies looked at one another.

'A-tishoo!' wept poor Tag. 'I sh-shall have to use my w-w-wish to t-take this ice-c-cream, because it is so dreadfully cold and it's f-freezing my neck all the time it drips. Oh, dear, what a waste of a wish!'

'Never mind,' said Bobtail, feeling very sorry for his brother. 'Wish it, Tag. Quick, before you get a dreadful cold in your head!'

'I wish – a-tishoo – that this ice-cream would go away!' said poor Tag. At once the ice-cream disappeared, and Tag wiped away a few drops from his neck. He sneezed once more and then sat down on a stool.

The three pixies looked at one another. They could hear the wise woman chuckling away to herself in the back room, and they grew very red, for they guessed she was laughing at them.

'She said that bad-tempered people should never have wishes to wish,' said Bobtail, sadly. 'And it's true. Look at us! We could have been happy, rich and loved by everyone – and instead of that we are just three silly, poor, hard-working and quarrelsome little pixies.'

'We can't help being poor and hard-working,' said Rag, 'but we *can* help being silly and quarrelsome. Let's cure our bad temper and be nice to one another. Then next time we have wishes to wish we shall use them properly and have everything we want!'

So they are trying very hard to be good and kind to one another, in case Lady Grumble one day *might* give them another chance. But I don't somehow think she will!

The Little Paper Boats

One night, when Paul and Mary were fast asleep, someone came knocking at their bedroom window.

'Tap!' went the noise. 'Tap-tap! Tap!'

Mary woke up first, and thought it was the wind blowing a branch against the window. Then she thought it wasn't, because it did sound so exactly like someone knocking. So she woke Paul up.

'Doesn't it sound as if someone is outside?' she whispered. 'Do you suppose it is a pixie?'

'Let's look!' said Paul and he jumped out of bed to see. The moon shone brightly outside – and what *do* you think he saw? Standing on the window-sill was a tiny creature dressed in silver, and she was tapping with her hand on the pane. 'Tap-tap! Tap!'

'It *is* a pixie or an elf!' cried Paul, in delight. He opened the window and the tiny creature climbed in.

'Oh, do forgive my waking you,' she said. 'But a dreadful thing has happened.'

'What?' cried both children.

'Well, you know the stream that runs to the bottom of your garden?' said the pixie. 'We were going to meet the Fairy Queen on the opposite side tonight, because she is going to hold a meeting there – and we had our pixie ship all ready to take us across. But a big wind blew suddenly and broke the rope that tied our ship to the shore. So now we can't get across because the ship has floated away, and we *are* so upset.'

'Oh, what a pity!' said Mary. 'Can we help you?'

'That's what I came to ask you,' said the pixie. 'Could you lend us a toy boat to sail across in?'

'We did have one,' said Paul, 'but it's broken. Its sail is gone, and it floats all on one side. I'm afraid it wouldn't be a bit of use to you.'

'Oh dear!' said the pixie, looking ready to burst into tears. 'Isn't that too bad? We felt quite sure you would have one. Have you anything else that would do?'

'No, I'm afraid not,' said Paul, trying to think of something. 'We've no raft, and not even a little penny rowing-boat. I *am* sorry!'

'Well, never mind,' said the pixie, climbing out to the window-sill. 'We shall just have to stay on this side of the stream and hope that the Queen will not be too cross with us. We have no wings, you see, or we could fly across.'

Mary suddenly clapped her hands. 'I know!' she cried. 'I know! What about some paper boats, pixie? Paul and I can make nice paper boats that will float on the water. They don't last very long but they would take you across the stream all right, I'm sure. Shall we make you some?'

'Oh, will you?' asked the pixie, in delight. 'That *is* kind of you! Thank you so much!'

'That's a good idea of yours, Mary,' said Paul. 'Quick, let's put on our dressing-gowns and go down to the stream with the pixie. We can take a newspaper with us and make as many boats as they like.'

So they put on their dressing-gowns, took an old newspaper from the cupboard, and then ran downstairs and out into the garden. The pixie met them there and they all three went down to the little stream that ran at the foot of the garden.

What a sight the two children saw! The moon shone brightly down on a crowd of little silvery creatures, dressed in misty gowns. They had tiny pointed faces and little high voices like swallows twittering. They were astonished to see the children and ran helter-skelter to hide. But the pixie that came with Paul and Mary called them back.

'It's quite safe,' she cried. 'These children are going to help us. They will make us some boats.'

'A small boat will take one or two of you,' said Paul. 'We'll make some of all sizes – and then some of you can go in crowds and some can go in twos and threes, just as you like.'

He and Mary began to tear the paper into oblongs, and then, very quickly, they folded their paper into this shape and that, until at last there came a little paper boat. The pixies

watched them in delight. They had never seen such a thing before.

Paul and Mary soon put two boats on the water, and two or three pixies clambered in. The boat went rocking up and down on the stream, and the pixies guided it towards the opposite bank. They screamed with delight as it went, and all the pixies left on shore begged

Paul and Mary to hurry up and make some more boats for them. Very soon there was a whole fleet of the little paper boats on the stream and the pixies sprang into them in joy. Across to the opposite shore they sailed one by one and landed safely on the opposite side.

The last pixie left was the one who had tapped on the bedroom window. Mary made her a dear little boat for herself and the pixie stepped into it.

'Good-bye,' she said. 'Don't wait here any longer, in case you catch cold. It's been so kind of you to help us. If you find our ship you may keep it for your own. It's a dear little ship, and we'd like you to have it.'

The children waved good-bye and then

went indoors to bed, talking excitedly of all that had happened. They thought that they were much too excited to go to sleep, but it wasn't long before they were dreaming, their heads cuddled into their pillows.

The next day they were quite certain they had dreamt it all, and they were surprised to find that they had both had the same dream – but they really didn't think they *could* have seen pixies in the night. It didn't seem real in the morning.

But what do you think they found later on in the day, when they went for a walk down by their stream? The little ship belonging to the pixies! There it was, caught in some rushes, a little silver-sailed ship with the name 'Silver Pixie' on its hull! Then they knew that their dream was true, and in great delight they rushed home to show their mother what they had found.

They keep the ship on the nursery mantelpiece because it is so pretty – and there it is to this day, a little glittering, silver ship! It sails beautifully, and you should see all the children stare when Paul and Mary take it down to the pond to sail!

I'd love to see it, wouldn't you?

The Cat and the Wishing-Well

There was once a little boy who was most unkind to animals. He threw stones at birds, he chased dogs and he caught cats and tied tin cans to their tails. So you can guess that all the animals and birds around his home feared him and hated him.

His mother was angry with him.

'One day, Tim,' she said, 'you will be very sorry for your horrid mischief. How would *you* like to be chased, or have tin-cans tied to you?'

'Pooh!' said Tim. 'I shouldn't mind at all!'

Now it happened that the very next day Tim chased the next-door cat and frightened the poor creature so much that it fell down the well at the bottom of the garden. Tim roared with laughter, but he didn't go to help the cat. No, he left the poor thing to get out as best it could.

The cat swam to the side of the well, and held on to the loose bricks with its claws. 'How I wish that I could do to Tim all the things he does to me and to the dogs and birds!' thought the cat.

The animal did not know that the well was a wishing-well! Whatever you wished when drawing water from the well, came true – and if anyone wished a wish right inside the well, the wish came true at once.

And so the cat's wish came true! As soon as someone came to draw water, the cat climbed into the bucket and was hauled safely to the top of the well, wet and shivering. She felt queer, because she was full of magic. She hopped on to the brick wall round the well and began to lick herself.

Tim was playing in the garden next door. He took up a stone and threw it at a sparrow. The cat lifted her head, and, much surprised at herself, said in a loud voice: 'Birds, throw stones at Tim!'

At once all the sparrows, thrushes, black-birds, robins and starlings picked up stones in their beaks and dropped them on Tim! He was frightened and astonished to find big and little stones dropping on his bare head.

He ran away – and the cat saw him and cried out: 'Dogs! Chase this boy as he has so many times chased you!'

At once all the dogs around jumped up and

ran after Tim. He tore away, yelling with fear, but nobody came to his help. The dogs rushed after him, and one of them nipped his fat leg. Another jumped and bit his thumb. This was a dog that Tim had beaten with a stick and he was glad to punish the horrid little boy.

'Now, cats, it's your turn!' cried the cat on the well. 'Find some old tin cans on the rubbish-heap and tie them to his coat! Then make him run and see how he likes the horrible clanking noise behind him!'

At once about eight cats of all sizes and colours rushed to the rubbish-heap and found some old tins. They carried them to the corner where the dogs were snarling at Tim and between them they fastened the tins by string to the boy's coat. Then the dogs set him running again, and when poor Tim heard the awful clinking-clanking noise behind him, he was more frightened than ever, and tore on faster and faster.

The cans flew off, one after another, as they banged against the road. But Tim still ran, frightened out of his life, chased by half the dogs and cats in the town. At last he stumbled up to the old well and leaned against it, panting.

'Let's push him in!' cried the first cat. 'He pushed *me* in! Let's push *him* in!'

'No, no!' begged Tim, frightened. 'No, please, please don't. I've learnt my lesson. I know what it is to be hurt and frightened. I didn't know before. I'll never, never throw stones again or chase you or be unkind. I'll always be good and careful with animals.'

'Well,' said a little brown dog to the cat,

'shall we let him? Once he gave me a drink of water when I was thirsty – so for the sake of that one kind deed, shall we let him go?'

'Very well,' said the cat, licking herself, 'for the sake of that one kind deed. It's a good thing he did *one* kind act in his life!'

'I'll do heaps more now!' promised Tim,

sobbing. 'I'd no idea how horrid I'd been to you. I didn't think. But I'm going to be different now. Let me lie down here in the sunshine and rest. My legs are so tired and I am full of bumps where the stones hit me.'

So the animals allowed him to lie down and fall asleep. The birds flew back to the trees and forgot about him. The dogs went back to their kennels, yawning. The cats lay down in the sun and slept. Only the cat that had fallen down the well was awake – but she soon settled down in the sun and fell asleep too, dreaming with delight of how she had punished that horrid boy, Tim.

When she awoke the magic had gone out of her. She was just an ordinary cat, and she had forgotten all about her wish that had come true. Tim woke up too – but he hadn't forgotten. He sat up and wondered if he had dreamt it all. But there were bumps and bruises on his head and arms, so he thought it must really have happened.

He went back home, thinking hard. He saw a cat on a wall, and to that animal's great surprise he stroked it! He met a dog and patted it! The dog was astonished, and licked Tim's hand. Tim was pleased to feel its little pink tongue.

'I've learnt my lesson,' he thought. 'Oh dear, what a dreadful dream that was! Or was it a dream? I really don't know!'

Tim's mother couldn't think what had happened to Tim after that. He put crumbs out for the birds. He bought a little tin trough and kept it full of water for dogs to drink in the hot weather. He brought home a stray cat that somebody had left behind and begged his mother to keep it.

'Well, you're a different boy, Tim!' said his mother, pleased. 'Goodness knows what's happened to you! Perhaps the dogs and cats treated you as you used to treat them and taught you a lesson. Something's changed you, anyway!'

Tim didn't tell his mother what had happened – he was much too ashamed – but he told me his story to tell to you, and that's how I know all about it. Wasn't it a strange thing to happen?

The Surprising Hoop-Sticks

Once upon a time there were two little gnomes called Tups and Twinkle. They were very fond of all kinds of toys, and they had beautiful sailing-ships, fine spinning-tops, big kites and all sorts of things.

They were very pleased with themselves one day because they had made two hoops. You should have seen those hoops! They were as big as the gnomes themselves and they were painted all sorts of colours. Tied to the inside edge of the hoops were tiny bells that rang when the hoops were bowled along.

All the gnomes were busy making hoops for themselves as soon as they saw those of Tups and Twinkle. What a tinkling and jingling

there was in Heigho Village when all the
hoops were set rolling!

'Let's have a Grand Hoop-Race,' said Tups
one day to the others. 'That would be fun. We
could start at one end of the village and finish
up at the other.'

'That's a good idea,' said all the gnomes. So

they made plans for a great hoop-race, and the
prize was to be three gold pennies to spend at
the cake-shop and at the sweet-shop.

Tups and Twinkle practised bowling their
hoops every morning and evening, for they
meant to win the prize.

'We could have peppermints from the
sweet-shop and currant buns from the cake-

shop every day for a year if we won the prize,'
said Tups.

'I wish we could be quite sure of winning it,'
said Twinkle. 'I wish we could get some hoop-
sticks that would bowl our hoops faster than
anyone else's.'

Twinkle looked at Tups and Tups looked at
Twinkle. Then they sat down and thought
hard, and it wasn't long before Tups had a
bright idea.

'I say, Twinkle!' he said. 'I know what
we'll do. We'll go to Wizard Too-Wise's
garden after supper tonight, when it's dark,
and we'll cut ourselves two nice strong hoop-
sticks from the wishing-tree in his front garden.
Then we'll use them for our hoops on the race
day and we'll be sure to win the prize!'

So that night when it was dark the two
naughty gnomes went along to Wizard Too-
Wise's house. They knew exactly where the
wishing-tree was, and it didn't take them long
to cut themselves two fine sticks from it. Then
off they went – but the gate creaked as they
went out and the wizard heard it.

'Robbers!' he cried, looking out of the
window. 'Thieves! Burglars! May whatever
you steal bring you back to me to punish!'

'Ooh!' said Tups and Twinkle, running away as fast as they could. 'We were nearly caught!'

They hadn't heard what the wizard said, and they would have been very much worried if they had; for his magic was powerful and never failed. They soon forgot their fright and put away their new hoop-sticks in the cupboard to wait for the great hoop-race.

The day came at last, and proudly the two little gnomes took their hoops to the edge of the village to join all the others. What a number of hoops there were! Green ones, blue ones, red, yellow, purple and orange ones, and some like Tups' and Twinkle's, all colours of the rainbow with little bells inside.

The two gnomes had their new hoop-sticks from the wizard's wishing-tree. They hadn't used them yet. They were busy wishing that their hoop-sticks should make their hoops go faster than any other gnome's so that they would be sure to win the prize.

Off they all went. Tap-tap-tap went the hoop-sticks on the rolling hoops. Down the winding village street ran a score of panting gnomes with their bright hoops, and far in front of everyone were Tups and

Twinkle, their hoops tinkling merrily as they ran.

'We shall win!' shouted Tups to Twinkle. 'Aren't our new sticks wonderful? They make our hoops go like the wind!'

But dear me, what a peculiar thing happened when the race was over! Tups and Twinkle won easily, and just as the prize was being given to them, something curious happened. Their feet and hands bent over and joined one another, and in a trice they were rolling over and over just like hoops! They were like big wheels rolling along – and oh, dear me, what was this that the hoop-sticks were doing?

The sticks leapt up in the air and began to hit the rolling, bowling gnomes, driving them along fast! Smack! Smack! Smack! How those

sticks hurt when they hit the rolling gnomes! Tups and Twinkle shouted in pain and fright, and all the other gnomes looked on in amazement.

Back up the village street went the bowling gnomes, rolling along merrily in the dust, the two magic hoop-sticks hitting them hard all the time. At last they came to Wizard Too-Wise's house and the gnomes rolled in at the gate, the hoop-sticks behind them.

Wizard Too-Wise was watering his wishing-tree and when he saw the two gnomes coming in at his gate, rolling up his garden path, he set down his can and roared till the tears ran down his cheeks. The gnomes had never seen him laugh so much before.

'So here are the thieves come back to me!' he said at last. 'Dear, dear, dear, what a very comical sight! So you thought you would get magic hoop-sticks, did you, and win the prize by cheating? Well, well, this is a very good punishment for you. Would you like to keep your magic hoop-sticks, Tups and Twinkle? They will be very pleased to bowl you anywhere you want to go.'

'Oh no, no,' said the gnomes, weeping bitterly. 'Take them away, and please, please, forgive us. We were very wrong. We will never cheat again. We might have won the prize if we had used our own hoop-sticks, but now we have lost it, and have been bowled all round the village for everyone to see. We are very bruised and ashamed. Please forgive us and let us go.'

The wizard said a few words and the hoop-sticks flew back to the wishing-tree and grew there again as branches. The gnomes found themselves able to stand upright, and, very red in the face, they walked back home, dusty, dirty and bruised.

'We will never, never cheat again in anything we do,' they said solemnly to one another.

And you may be quite sure they never, never did!

The Little Pinching Girl

Nobody liked Elsie, because she was always pinching people. Wasn't it horrid of her? At school she pinched the little boy who sat next to her and made him cry out. At home she pinched her little sister and the twins next door. When she went out to play she pinched the children near to her, and they didn't like it at all.

Elsie's mother was cross with her.

'Why don't you stop pinching people?' she said. 'They don't like it, because it hurts them. You are a very unkind child, Elsie, to pinch others. It is a stupid habit and you must stop it, or you will be very sorry.'

But Elsie didn't stop. She pinched Joan, and she pinched Tom. She pinched Alan, and she pinched Willie – but she didn't pinch Big Mary, because Big Mary could slap very hard. She really was a very horrid little girl.

And then one day something happened. She went down to the seaside for her Sunday School treat. It was great fun, because all the children went in motor-coaches, and they were very much excited about it. Elsie was so excited that she pinched children all the way, so that nobody wanted to sit next to her. But somebody had to, of course, so Elsie always had some poor child to pinch.

When they arrived at the seaside they all went to the sands and sat down to eat their dinner. Elsie was hungry and she soon finished hers. Afterwards she felt sleepy and she lay down by a big sand-castle and shut her eyes.

She hadn't shut them for more than a moment when she heard voices not far from her.

'This must be our dear little friend,' said one of the voices. 'How nice it is to see her!'

'Yes, this is Elsie,' said another voice. 'We must shake hands with her and tell her how very pleased we are to see her.'

Elsie opened her eyes and sat up with a jerk. Who was talking?

She saw a very queer sight. Two large lobsters were sitting against the sand-castle, looking at her with broad smiles on their funny faces. She stared at them in astonishment.

'Oh, good morning, Elsie,' said one of the lobsters, holding out a great pincer-paw to the surprised little girl. 'We are *so* pleased to see you. We know you are a great friend of ours.'

Elsie put out her hand to shake the lobster's

claw – and how she shouted and yelled! The lobster was pinching her fingers in its trap-like claw, and wouldn't let go.

'Let go!' shouted Elsie, with tears in her eyes. 'Oh, you horrid creature, you're hurting me!'

'But I'm only pinching you,' said the lobster in surprise. 'You are very fond of pinching, aren't you? That is why we are so pleased to welcome you here as our dear little friend. We are fond of pinching too.'

'Will you let my hand go?' wept Elsie, trying to take her hand away from the lobster's great claw. At last he let it go, and the little girl nursed her pinched hand and glared angrily at the big lobster. The other lobster leaned forward and held *his* claw to shake hands. But Elsie wouldn't touch it.

'No, you horrid creature,' she said. 'I'm not going to have my hand pinched again!'

'How impolite you are not to shake hands with me!' said the lobster, shocked. He came closer to Elsie and took hold of her arm. Dear me, how he pinched with his big claws! Elsie screamed and tried to shake off his claw, but she couldn't.

'What's the matter, now, what's the matter?' asked the lobster, surprised. 'You're a pincher, aren't you? You love pinching, I know, so why do you make such a fuss when you meet two nice pinchers like ourselves? We thought you would be very pleased to see us.'

'Well, I'm not, then,' said Elsie, wishing with all her heart that she had never pinched anyone in her life.

'Perhaps she will be better pleased to meet

our cousins the crabs,' said the first lobster. 'Here they come.'

Elsie saw about a dozen crabs hurrying up the beach, some large and some small, all waving their pincer-like claws to her as they came scuttling up sideways.

They crowded round her and soon began to nip her bare legs and toes.

'Ooh!' cried Elsie, trying to get her legs safely under her. 'Stop nipping me, you horrid little things!'

The crabs looked at her in astonishment.

'Aren't you a pincher too?' they asked. 'We thought you were the little girl who loves pinching.'

'Well, I don't like *being* pinched,' wept Elsie. 'Do go away.'

'Why don't you pinch *us*?' said the crabs. 'You can pinch us back, you know. We expect it.'

Elsie tried to pinch a crab very hard. But it had a thick shell and it didn't mind a bit. It caught hold of her thumb and nipped it.

'This is a fine game!' cried the crabs and lobsters excitedly. 'Come on, Elsie – you try to pinch us, and we'll try to pinch you!'

But it wasn't a fair game, because Elsie's

hands and legs were soft and it hurt her to be pinched. The crabs and lobsters all wore hard shells and they couldn't be pinched. Elsie kicked at them and tried to knock them away.

'Don't you like us?' said the big lobsters sadly. 'We did so look forward to your coming to the seaside. We thought it would be so nice to welcome another member of the pinching

family. Do play with us, Elsie. You pinch other children hundreds of times a day – why can't you play at pinching with us?'

'I'm never never going to pinch anyone again,' wept Elsie. 'I didn't know it could be so horrid. I don't belong to your nasty pinching family. I'm going to be a nice kind little girl who doesn't pinch or slap or pull hair. I'm ashamed of myself for being like crabs and lobsters, so there!'

When the crabs and lobsters heard her

saying this they all cried out in horror and scuttled down the shore to the sea as fast as ever they could.

'She's not a friend of ours!' they shouted. 'She isn't a pincher any more!'

Elsie wiped her eyes with her handkerchief and looked round. Someone was coming towards her. It was her Sunday School teacher.

'Come along and play, Elsie!' she cried. 'Have you been asleep?'

'No,' said Elsie, scrambling to her feet. 'But I've had a very nasty adventure. Do you know, some crabs and lobsters came and told me I belonged to their nasty pinching family, and they wanted me to play pinching each other with them. And I told them I'm never going to pinch anyone again.'

'I'm very glad,' said her teacher. 'People will like you much better if you are kind and gentle.'

Elsie has never pinched anyone from that day – and the other children don't mind sitting next to her now. I'm glad *I* don't pinch people, aren't you? I wouldn't like to play with crabs and lobsters at all!

The Tale of Flop and Whiskers

Flop and Whiskers were two white rabbits belonging to Malcolm and Jean. They had fine whiskers, little black bobtails and big floppy ears. Malcolm and Jean were very fond of them and looked after them well.

Flop and Whiskers lived happily enough in a big cage. They were friendly with one another, but sometimes they found things dull.

'Oh, if only something exciting would happen!' Flop would sigh.

'Yes, something that we could remember and talk about for weeks and weeks,' said Whiskers. 'But nothing ever happens to pet rabbits. They just live in a cage and eat and sleep. That's all.'

But one night something *did* happen! Flop and Whiskers heard a noise in the garden, and looked out of their cage. It was bright moonlight and coming down the garden path was a long procession of fairies. In their midst was a snow-white carriage with gold handles and gold wheels. It was drawn by six coal-black rabbits.

'Just look at that!' cried Flop, excitedly. 'It must be a fairy princess of some kind. Oh, don't I wish I was one of those rabbits pulling her carriage! Wouldn't I feel grand!'

'Isn't it beautiful?' said Whiskers, his little nose pressed against the wires of the cage.

The procession came down the path and passed by the rabbits' cage. They were so excited. They could see a golden-haired princess in the snow-white carriage and just as

she passed their cage she leaned out and blew a kiss to them. Flop scraped at the wire of the cage, trying her hardest to get out and run after the procession – but it was no use, the wire was too strong.

'Look!' suddenly cried Whiskers. 'The procession has stopped. What has happened?'

'One of the coal-black rabbits has gone lame,' said Flop. 'See, its foot is limping.'

What a to-do there was! All the fairies gathered round the limping rabbit, who shook his head dolefully and held up his foot in pain.

The princess leaned out of her carriage and pointed to the rabbit-hutch she had just passed. She called out something in her high little voice.

'I say, Flop, I believe the princess is saying that one of us could draw her carriage instead of the lame rabbit!' said Whiskers, in excitement. 'Oh, I wonder which of us will be chosen.'

The little fairies came running back to the cage and climbed up to the wire.

'Will you come and draw our princess's carriage just for tonight?' they cried. 'One of our rabbits has hurt its foot.'

'Oh yes!' squeaked the two white rabbits in delight. 'But which of us do you want?'

'Both of you, please,' said the fairies. 'You see, the rabbits have to go in pairs, and we couldn't make one of the pairs a black rabbit and a white one. We shall set free the hurt rabbit and his companion, so that we can have two white rabbits instead. So will you both come? You shall be brought back before sunrise.'

Flop and Whiskers joyfully told the fairies how to open their cage and then they jumped out in delight. In a trice they were harnessed with the other rabbits, and the two black ones, whose place they were taking, hopped away into the hedges. The fairies cried out in delight to see the two beautiful white rabbits among the coal-black ones.

They made such a noise that they woke up Malcolm and Jean. The children jumped out of bed and went to their bedroom window, looking out into the moonlight.

They saw the fairy procession going along down the garden path and they stared in astonishment.

'Jean!' said Malcolm, 'look at those two white rabbits with black tails, drawing the carriage along with the four black rabbits. Don't they look like Flop and Whiskers.'

'Yes, they do,' said Jean. 'And oh, look! Malcolm, their cage door is open. I can see it quite plainly in the moonlight.'

The children ran downstairs to see the procession, but it had passed by before they were

in the garden. So they went to see if the rabbit-cage was open – and it was.

'Oh dear, I *shall* be sorry not to have dear old Flop and Whiskers,' said Jean, almost crying. 'They were so sweet. I don't think it was very kind of the fairies to take them away from us.'

But the next morning the cage door was fast shut and the two white rabbits were safely back in their hutch once more! When Malcolm and Jean went to peep, they found both rabbits fast asleep in the hay, and they didn't even wake when the children put some fresh lettuce in for them.

'Goodness, aren't they tired!' said Jean. 'I expect they walked for miles last night, dragging that lovely carriage behind them. I do wonder where they went.'

Where *did* they go? Well, they went to a party! The Prince of Derry-Down Palace was just twenty-one and he had sent out invitations to his birthday party – and, of course, the golden-haired Princess had one of the beautiful invitation cards too.

Her name was Fenella, and she loved parties. She had only just grown up, so she hadn't been to many big parties. She had a new dress and new silver shoes made, and she looked very lovely in them.

'I will lend you my second-best coach, the white one with gold wheels,' said her father, the King. 'And you shall have either my six well-matched coal-black rabbits to draw it, or my six white cats with pink eyes.'

The Princess chose the rabbits, and they were the very ones that the two children had seen in the night. The two white rabbits, Flop and Whiskers, watched the two black ones whose place they took, run into the hedge, and then off they went with the other four.

'I hope we keep up all right,' panted Flop. 'We aren't very used to galloping, we've been so used to sitting in our cage.'

But they galloped along just as fast as the black rabbits, and the Princess was very pleased. 'They shall go to the Rabbits' Party,' she said to the fairies with her. 'They deserve it.'

The Prince was giving a party for his friends and the rabbits he sometimes rode were giving a party for the six rabbits who drew the Princess's coach – so you can imagine the delight of Flop and Whiskers when four fine rabbits with bows round their necks, made them welcome to their own little party in the grounds of the palace!

They were given blue bows to wear, and sat down at little tables with dishes of delicious looking food.

'Look, Flop,' said Whiskers. 'Carrot Sandwiches!'

'And see – that's Cabbage Pie!' said Flop. 'And here's Turnip Cake. And what's this – Lettuce Biscuits! What a wonderful meal!'

It certainly was – and afterwards the ten rabbits had a little dance of their own. Flop and Whiskers were very sorry when it was all over. They pulled the Princess's carriage home for her – and then they ran back to their cage and curled up to go to sleep, tired out!

Flop and Whiskers longed to tell the children all about their adventures, but they couldn't. When they woke up they looked at one another in delight, and Flop said: 'Did we dream it, Whiskers, or was it true?'

'Quite true,' said Whiskers. 'We've had an adventure at last, Flop. We can talk about it for weeks and weeks, and we'll never feel dull again.'

So they talk about it all day long – and I wish I could listen to them, don't you?

Peter's Horrid Afternoon

Peter wanted a bicycle. He wanted one very badly indeed, so badly that he made up his mind to be a very good, kind, unselfish boy for weeks. Then he hoped that his mother would buy him a bicycle.

It wasn't very difficult for Peter to be kind and unselfish, for he was a good-hearted boy and always willing to do a good turn for anyone. His mother didn't really notice very much difference, for Peter was always good to her. But Peter was hoping and hoping that she would notice how hard he was trying to be good so that she would give him a reward.

One day, after he had been trying hard for about four weeks, he asked his mother a question.

'Do you think I deserve a bicycle, Mother?' he asked.

'Deserve a bicycle!' said his mother in surprise. 'What for?'

'Well, haven't I been good as can be all these weeks?' said Peter. 'I thought you would be sure to notice. Didn't you?'

'Well, no, I didn't,' said his mother. She was just about to say that Peter was *always* a kind-hearted boy, but he didn't give her time. He went very red and looked quite cross and upset.

'Well, really, Mother!' he said, 'I don't see any use in my trying so hard if nobody is going to notice. You did once say that if I were a very specially good boy you might think of buying me a bicycle, and now I expect you've forgotten all about it! It's no use being kind! It's no use being good! I just won't be any more!'

Peter's mother was so astonished that she couldn't say a word. Peter walked out of the room and went into the garden. He felt very cross and disappointed. It was too bad to have tried so hard for so long and then to be told that his mother hadn't even noticed he was any better. He didn't guess it was because he was always such a kindly boy that his mother hadn't noticed anything different about him.

'I'll go for a walk all by myself,' thought Peter, half-sulky with his disappointment. 'I'll go up on the common, past the police-station and down by the sweet-shop. And I won't do a kind deed to anyone, and I won't smile or say good afternoon. I'll just be simply horrid and see if anyone notices *that*!'

So, much to everyone's surprise, Peter went frowning through the village and didn't raise his cap to anyone or say good afternoon. He saw old Mrs. Harrison coming and because he didn't want to shake hands with her and be his usual kind self he turned his back on her and pretended to read a notice outside the police-station.

It was quite an interesting notice, all about a robbery that had taken place in a big house not far away. Peter read about the things that had been stolen, and at the end it said that it was believed that the thieves had hidden the stolen things somewhere, and anyone finding them must report to the police.

'I wish *I* could find them!' thought Peter. 'It would be exciting. I'd like that. I'll look under the bushes on the common as I pass them. You never know what might happen!'

So he went on his way feeling a little happier. But when he passed Harry Brown, waving a brand-new kite to show him, he remembered that he was being horrid that afternoon and he scowled and looked away. Harry was so surprised.

He was soon up on the common. A little girl threw a ball near to him and asked him to throw it back – but Peter took no notice at all

and stalked on, his hands in his pockets. He
WAS NOT going to be kind. It didn't pay.
Nobody noticed. He might as well be horrid!
Wasn't he being silly?

He passed by some goats and a little kid
tied to a post. The rope had got wound round

one of its legs and Peter saw it. He was just
going to run over and free it when he remembered that he was being horrid. No, he must
leave the kid as it was. On he went, scowling
all round, looking under the bushes as he
passed. But there was no sack of stolen things
anywhere. Only dead leaves lay under the
bushes.

Then he suddenly heard the sound of someone crying. He looked about and saw Pam, a little girl he knew. She was weeping bitterly, and when she saw him she ran to him.

'Oh, Peter, Peter!' she cried. 'Will you help me? I've dropped my doll down this big hole here, and I can't get it back.'

Peter badly wanted to help her, but he remembered that he was being horrid.

'I'm sorry,' he said, 'I'm not doing any kind deeds today. I can't get your doll.'

'Oh, Peter, please, please do!' sobbed Pam. 'I do want her so. I can't leave her there. I'll have to climb down myself and I'm afraid.'

Peter looked at the little girl and then he suddenly thought it was a nasty thing to be horrid to people. He didn't care whether he had a reward or not – he was going to be good and kind whatever happened! He wanted to be. It didn't matter if he had a bicycle or anything else for being good – he could be kindly without that. How could he let Pam climb down that big crack in the earth and get her doll? She might break her leg!

He went to the hole where she said her doll had fallen. There was a great crack in the common just there and a large and jagged hole ran down into the earth. Bushes grew here and there in the crack, which was steep and dangerous. But Peter wanted to help Pam so he began to climb down.

He could see the doll's blue dress not very far down and he soon reached it – and then, just as he was about to climb up again, he caught sight of something else poked into a hole nearby. It looked like an old sack! Peter pulled at it and it came away from its hiding-place. He slid down a little further and opened the sack. Inside were all the things that had been stolen by the thieves when they had robbed the big house!

Peter felt so excited that he could hardly speak. At last he found his tongue. 'Pam!' he cried. 'Isn't it exciting! I believe I've found all the things those robbers stole the other night! Quick! We'll go and tell the police where they are. The sack is too heavy for me to pull up.'

He climbed out of the crack and he and Pam set off as fast as they could run to the police-station. They told a policeman what they had found, and very soon all three were going back to the hole again – and sure enough the sack of stolen goods was there! The policeman was pleased, and took it away on his back. Pam was excited too, and as for Peter, he could hardly go home fast enough, he was so eager to tell his mother all about it.

All the stolen goods were sent back to the

owner, and when he heard who had found them, he called at Peter's house to give him a reward.

'I offered five pounds to anyone who could tell me where my goods were hidden by the thieves,' he said to Peter's mother. 'Would Peter like the money, do you think, or would he rather have a present?'

'He is at school just now,' said his mother,

'but if you would like to give him a present, I know what he would like – a bicycle!'

'He shall have one!' said the man at once. 'I'll buy him one today.' And that afternoon what should Peter see waiting for him in the garden but the brightest, newest, finest bicycle he had ever imagined! He was simply delighted. Then he went rather red and looked at his mother.

'You know, Mother,' he said, 'I was being very silly and horrid that afternoon. I just wouldn't be kind or polite to anyone – but when I saw Pam so miserable I *had* to help her – and that's how I found the stolen goods.'

'Ah, Peter, you see you were rewarded for your kindness after all,' said his mother smiling. 'It is always best to be kind, for somehow and some time kindness brings its own reward – though you don't need to think about that. Now go and ride your bicycle.'

'I shall give Pam the first ride!' said Peter. 'If she hadn't dropped her doll down that hole I would never have found the sack! So she deserves the first ride!'

Off he went – and isn't he proud of that bright new bicycle! I would be too, wouldn't you?

The Palace of Bricks

Donald and Mary had a big box of bricks between them. The bricks were all colours, and there were so many that the two children could build really big houses, castles and palaces.

One sunny day Mummy said they could take their bricks out into the garden and build there. She gave them a big flat piece of cardboard to build on, and Mary carried that out, whilst Donald took the box of bricks.

'Let's build a palace today,' said Donald. 'We've got all afternoon to build it. There's a fine palace in the book that goes with the bricks – look! It shows you just what bricks to use, and how to make the towers and pinnacles on top of the palace.'

So they began. It was very difficult, but perfectly lovely to do. They had to find all the right bricks, and put them in just the right places. The palace began to grow and when Mummy came out to look, she thought it was grand!

'It's fit for a Princess,' she said. 'It really is.'

They finished it just after tea. It stood out there in the garden, with all its little towers rising gracefully, the prettiest palace you would imagine!

Just as they had finished it Mummy called them.

'Donald! Mary! Here is Peter come to ask you to go and try his new see-saw!'

Donald and Mary left their palace of bricks and rushed to the front garden, where Peter stood waiting.

'Are you coming?' he asked. 'I've made a fine new see-saw out of a tree-trunk and a big plank.'

Off they all rushed and that was the last that Donald and Mary remembered of their palace before they went to bed that night! They had a fine time with Peter's see-saw and got back home so late that Mummy bundled them into bed at once. And nobody thought of the bricks left out-of-doors!

Now it began to rain heavily after the children were in bed, but they were asleep and didn't know. Outside in the darkness the palace of bricks stood, getting wetter and wetter. Soon, down the garden there shone many little lanterns, and the sound of high voices could be heard. The little sparrows roosting in the trees heard them and whispered to one another: 'It's the pixie-folk! They were going to have a party tonight! What a pity the rain will spoil it!'

It *did* spoil the party! The pixies were terribly upset, especially as it was a birthday party for the little Princess Peronel.

'Whatever shall we do?' they cried, as they swung their lanterns here and there. 'The grass is much too wet to dance on, and all our cakes and jellies will be spoilt!'

'What's this?' suddenly cried a small pixie in yellow, running up to the palace of bricks. 'I say! Look at this! It's a beautiful palace! Why, it's just the thing to have the party in!'

All the pixies crowded round to see the palace. They were delighted with it. They ran inside the door and looked round the big rooms.

'They're quite dry!' they cried. 'The palace

has a fine roof, and not a drop of rain is leaking through! Those children must have built it. Let's use it for our party!'

'Let's!' cried the Princess Peronel, peeping in too. 'I'd love to have a party here. Fetch the tables and the stools, and we'll soon have a fine time!'

It wasn't long before the palace was hung with shining lanterns, and set with little golden tables and stools. On the tables were all kinds of cakes, jellies and trifles, with little blue jugs of honey-lemonade to drink. The cardboard floor was soon polished up and the band took their places to play merry dance-tunes.

You should have seen inside that palace! It was perfectly lovely! The pixies were dancing together, talking at the tops of their little voices, and the Princess Peronel was sitting on a golden chair watching everyone with a happy smile on her face. The little lanterns shone brightly down, and nobody would ever have guessed that the palace was only built of toy bricks, and hadn't been made till that very afternoon.

Now the rain went on pouring down all night, and it pattered so hard against the children's window that at last it woke Donald and he sat up in bed. Then he suddenly remembered that they had left their bricks outside.

'Mary!' he said. 'Wake up! I say, aren't we silly, we've left that brick palace out-of-doors, and it's pouring with rain! It will all be spoilt in the morning, and Mummy will be so cross with us.'

'Oh dear!' said Mary, sitting up. 'Well, I know, Donald! Let's put on our dressing-gowns, with our mackintoshes over them, and our Wellington boots, and go out and get the bricks. It will be quite an adventure!'

So they quickly put on their dressing-gowns and their mackintoshes, and out they went into the dark garden. But when they came near the palace of bricks they stopped in the greatest astonishment.

'There are people inside!' whispered Mary. 'Look! It's all hung with lanterns! And there's a band playing!'

They stooped down and peeped into their palace. What an exciting sight they saw! They could hardly believe their eyes.

'Pixies!' said Donald. 'Pixies! Well, fancy that! We've always wanted to see fairies, and there they are, having a perfectly lovely time in our palace of bricks. What a good thing we left the bricks here!'

Suddenly one of the pixies gave a scream and pointed to the two children who were bending down to peep in at the windows.

'Look!' she cried. 'Oh, look! Quick, run away, everybody!'

'No, please don't,' said Donald, politely. 'We're very glad indeed to see you using our palace. We remembered that we had left it

outside in the rain so we came to put away the bricks – and we saw you. But please go on with your party!'

'Oh, do you mind?' asked the Princess Peronel, coming to the door and looking up at the children. 'It was such a wet night, we

couldn't dance out-of-doors – so when we found this perfectly lovely palace we thought we'd use it. But do you think the rain will hurt it?'

'Never mind if it does,' said Donald. 'We wouldn't dream of putting the bricks away now.'

'It's very kind of you,' said the Princess. 'I'll tell you what we'll do for you. We will send the sun brownies to dry every single bit of the palace at dawn, and when you come out in the morning, you will see it is all quite dry, and no harm will come to the bricks.'

'Thank you,' said Mary gratefully. 'That is very nice of you. Good night – we won't stay any longer because we're getting wet!'

Back to the bedroom they went, most excited, and they talked hard about their adventure until they fell asleep. In the morning they raced out to the garden.

There was their palace, as dry as could be, shining in the sunshine! Not a single brick was wet!

They told their mother all about it, but she laughed and said they must have dreamt it.

'We *couldn't* have dreamt it, could we, Mary?' said Donald as they slowly took down the palace to put away the bricks. 'Oh, I say – look here!'

He picked up a little golden dish of the tiniest cakes you could imagine!

'The pixies left these behind!' he said. 'Let's go and show Mummy! She'll believe us then.'

And she did! The two children are going to eat the cakes for their tea. I do wonder what will happen when they do, don't you?

Jeanie's Monkey

There was once upon a time a little girl called Jeanie, who had a great many pets. She had a dog called Pip, a cat called Whiskers, two guinea-pigs called Bubble and Squeak, and a small toad that lived under the garden step. So you see she had a great many creatures to look after.

What she longed to have was a little monkey! She thought it would be lovely to have a small brown monkey that would play with her and Pip. But her Mummy said no, she had quite enough pets.

One day Jeanie was lying on the grass playing with Whiskers, when she suddenly saw a four-leaved clover. Now these are very lucky, as you know, and Jeanie was delighted. She knew that if she tied it on a thread and wore it round her neck all day, she could wish a wish and it might come true. For four-leaved clovers are magic and belong to the fairies.

Jeanie picked the clover-leaf and looked at it carefully to make sure there was no mistake. It was quite right – it had four leaves as plain as anything. Jeanie ran indoors and showed her mother. Then she took a piece of black cotton and tied the clover-leaf carefully to it. She wore it round her neck the whole day long – and what do you suppose she wished?

'I wish I could have a little brown monkey,' she said to herself all day long, wishing as hard as she could.

But no monkey came. Jeanie was most disappointed and she went to bed thinking that four-leaved clovers couldn't be magic after all. And then, just as she was falling asleep, she heard a funny little sound in the day nursery, next to her bedroom.

She sat up and listened. It was a little chattering noise. Jeanie couldn't think *what* it could be!

'I'll go and see!' she thought, and she popped out of bed and ran into the day nursery. She *was* astonished at what she found there.

The chattering noise came from the corner where the doll's cot stood – and there, cuddling into the cot, was a small brown monkey!

'My dream's come true!' cried Jeanie in delight, and she ran across to the monkey. He put out a tiny paw, just like a hand and stroked her. Then he cuddled down into the doll's cot again. He was shivering with cold.

'You poor little thing!' cried Jeanie. 'You are so cold! I'll get you a woolly coat that belongs to my big teddy bear. That will keep you warm.'

So she got the warm red coat and put it on the monkey. He was so pleased. Then Jeanie tucked him up in the cot and told him to go to sleep till morning.

He cuddled down and closed his eyes. Jeanie ran back to bed, very happy. Her dream had come true. Four-leaved clovers were magic, after all!

Next morning she went to look for the monkey and found him still fast asleep in the cot. She wondered what he would like for his breakfast, and she remembered that monkeys like bananas. So she ran to the cupboard where Mummy kept the fruit and took a banana. She peeled it and put it on a plate. The little monkey soon woke up when she patted him, and sat up in the cot. He was delighted to see the banana, and took it off the plate.

'Chitter-chitter, chatter, chitter!' he said, in his little chattery voice. He held the banana in his paw and bit big pieces off it, looking at Jeanie with his bright eyes as he ate. She thought he was the dearest little monkey in the world.

'You look rather dirty,' she said. 'I think I will give you a good wash. And see – your hind

paw is hurt. I will wrap it up in a bandage for you.'

Just then Mummy called her to breakfast and she ran off. She chattered all about the monkey whilst she had her breakfast, but her mother thought she was talking about a toy monkey she had, and took no notice. Jeanie ran back after her breakfast and got her doll's bath ready. She filled it full of nice hot water and made it soapy. Then she got an old nail-brush and called the monkey. He came at once.

He didn't like the bath very much, but he

did look nice and clean afterwards. Jeanie scrubbed him with the nail-brush and then rubbed him dry with an old towel. She put on the little coat again, and tied a scarf round his neck. Then she put him down in the sun, and he fell asleep again. He really was a dear little monkey, and he seemed quite a baby one.

Before he fell asleep Jeanie bound up his paw, which was cut, and he was very pleased with the bandage. He kept looking at it until he fell asleep. Jeanie put him in her doll's pram and thought she would take him for a walk. She took him into the garden and walked round and round with him. When he woke up he was quite ready for a game.

You should have seen that monkey playing! He pulled Pip's tail, he climbed all the trees, he chattered to Whiskers, who was half afraid of him, and he kept jumping on to Jeanie's shoulder and pulling off her hair-slide.

He really was the most mischievous little creature!

When Mummy came out into the garden she stared in the greatest astonishment at the monkey. She really could hardly believe her eyes.

'Jeanie!' she cried. 'Where did that monkey come from?'

'It's the one I told you about at breakfast-time this morning,' said Jeanie.

'But I thought you were talking about your *toy* monkey then!' said her mother. 'Where did this little creature come from?'

'I wished for him and he came,' said Jeanie. 'I found a four-leaved clover, you see, Mummy.'

Well, her mother was as puzzled as could be. She kept saying that the monkey must have escaped from somewhere, and Jeanie really couldn't keep him. And Jeanie kept saying that it was *her* monkey because she had wished him and he had come.

When Cook saw the monkey she said she knew where he came from.

'I'm sure it's the monkey I saw on the barrel-organ belonging to the Italian who used to play down our street at home,' she said. 'I've often seen the cruel man beating him, poor little monkey. He's only a young monkey, and a gentle creature, too.'

'Well, we must find out if it *does* belong to the organ-grinder,' said Mummy. But Jeanie began to cry when she heard that.

'It's *my* monkey!' she said. 'It doesn't belong to the organ-grinder. I wished him and he came.'

But, you know, he *did* belong to the organ-grinder, because when Daddy began to try to find out about him, a policeman told him that the Italian had lost his monkey.

'Oh, he can't go back to that horrid man!' wept Jeanie, hugging the little monkey to her. 'I won't have him beaten, poor little thing. He's so gentle and sweet.'

'I'll go and see the organ-grinder and find out what he says,' said Daddy. So off he went. He soon found out where the man lived, and knocked at the door.

The Italian lived in two dirty little rooms,

and when he heard that his monkey had been found he wanted it back at once.

'It is a silly, weak animal,' he said. 'I do not like it. It has to be beaten every day because it will not learn to take round my hat for pennies.'

'Well, if you like I will buy it from you for my little girl,' said Daddy. 'She likes it, and it seems happy with her. If you take it back it will probably catch a cold and die.'

'You give me four shillings and you can have the silly little animal,' said the organ-grinder at once. Daddy paid him four shillings and went home. He called Jeanie as soon as he got back. She came running to him, hugging the little monkey, her eyes full of tears because she thought her Daddy was going to take it back to the organ-grinder.

'Cheer up, Jeanie,' said Daddy. 'The organ-grinder doesn't want the monkey. You can

keep it! Look after it well, for it is not very strong and has been badly treated.'

Well, you should have seen Jeanie's face! It was as bright as the sun! She hugged her Daddy, she hugged her Mummy, she hugged the monkey!

'I knew he was mine!' she cried. 'I wished him and he came. I knew he was mine! The fairies knew he was unhappy, so when they heard my monkey-wish, they took him away from the unkind organ-grinder and brought him to my nursery. They did, Mummy, truly, because you know I found a four-leaved clover, and that's magic! Oh, I am so glad to have him for a pet!'

The monkey still lives with Jeanie and Pip and Whiskers. You'll see him if ever you go to tea. He is a real little mischief, and he will take your handkerchief out of your pocket whenever you are not looking. So be careful when you play with him!

Thimble's Whirlwind

Once upon a time, in the village of Go-and-See there lived a big, fat gnome called Brin-Brin. He was very proud and haughty, always rude to everyone, and thought such a lot of himself, that nobody dared to speak to him unless he spoke first.

Next door to Brin-Brin lived a tiny pixie, called Thimble. He didn't like being next door to Brin-Brin at all. For one thing the big gnome threw all his rubbish over the wall into Thimble's garden, and he was always having to clear up tins, bottles and potato parings. It was a great nuisance. But he didn't like to complain.

Another thing was that Brin-Brin often used to sing very loudly, and as he had a dreadful voice, it was very painful for Thimble to have to sit and listen to it.

He would shut his windows to keep the sound out, but as soon as Brin-Brin saw him doing that he would sing twice as loudly as before, so it was really worse.

Thimble was a good-natured little pixie, and he would have liked to be friendly to Brin-Brin, but it was quite impossible. He really was a horrid person, and he ate so much that poor Thimble's garden was always full of rubbishy tins and pots thrown over the wall by the greedy gnome.

Thimble felt one day that he really could *not* put up with Brin-Brin any longer. So he sat on his three-legged stool and tried to think of a plan to get rid of him. It was very difficult – but at last he thought of one. He waited until a windy day came, and he watched for Brin-Brin to set out on his usual walk through Red-Leaf Woods.

Then he followed after him. Brin-Brin walked on, crunching the dead leaves under his feet, for it was autumn. Behind him came Thimble. Brin-Brin sat down at the foot of a tree and unwrapped a parcel of sticky buns that he was going to eat.

Thimble waited a little while behind another tree a little way off. Then he suddenly began to cry out loudly: 'Help! Help! There's a great, big whirlwind coming! Help! Help!'

Then Thimble started to run towards Brin-Brin as if there was a wind behind him, blowing him along. He shot by Brin-Brin, clutched hold of a tree and cried: 'Help! Help! There's a great big whirlwind coming! It nearly blew me away then.'

Brin-Brin was so astonished that he dropped two of his buns to the ground. He stared at Thimble in a great fright, his big mouth wide open. Once a whirlwind had come to the village of Go-and-See and had blown off all the chimney-pots, and ever since then Brin-Brin had been very much afraid of a storm.

'Oh, is that you, Brin-Brin!' shouted Thimble, pretending that he saw the gnome for the first time. 'You hold on to a tree like I'm doing! Quick! The whirlwind might come at any minute and blow you away to the moon!'

Brin-Brin jumped up, shaking like a jelly, and held on to the tree behind him. At the same moment a little wind blew the dry leaves about, and Brin-Brin shouted in terror, for he really thought it was the beginning of the whirlwind. He clung to his tree tightly.

'Oh, Brin-Brin,' said Thimble, 'what a pity you are so fat! The whirlwind will easily be able to take you away, and will bowl you along like a piece of paper. If you were small like me, you would be all right, for the wind would hardly notice you.'

'D-d-d-d-do you th-th-think s-s-so?' said

poor Brin-Brin, his teeth chattering so much that he could hardly talk. 'Oh, whatever shall I do? I shall never be able to hold on long enough to this tree.'

'I've a piece of rope here,' said Thimble, at once. 'Shall I tie you tightly to the tree? Then

the whirlwind won't be able to blow you away, however much it tries.'

'Oh, do, do!' begged Brin-Brin. 'Quick, before it starts!'

Thimble ran over to Brin-Brin. The wind blew a little again, and Brin-Brin gave a cry of fright.

'Quick! Tie me up! The whirlwind is beginning!'

Thimble grinned to himself, and very quickly he tied Brin-Brin to the tree. How tightly he tied him! You should have seen the knots. My goodness, they would have held an elephant!

'There!' said Thimble, stepping back to look at Brin-Brin. 'You're nicely tied up!'

'Come back and hold to a tree!' cried Brin-Brin. 'You'll be blown away.'

'Oh, *I'm* not afraid of a silly old whirlwind,' said Thimble, and to Brin-Brin's great astonishment he walked away, leaving the gnome alone.

But not for long! Oh no, there was soon

quite a crowd round Brin-Brin, for Thimble
had fetched all the village along to see him.

'However did you manage to conquer Brin-
Brin and tie him up like that?' cried all the
little folk. 'Did you fight him, Thimble? Oh,
how clever you are! How strong! How wonderful! Tell us all about it.'

'Oh, there's nothing to tell,' said Thimble
airily. 'Nothing at all. I thought it was time
that Brin-Brin was punished, so I tied him up
for everyone to see.'

Well, you should have seen Brin-Brin's face
when he heard all this! He simply didn't know
what to say!

'I'm tied up be-because there's a whirlwind
c-c-coming,' he said at last. 'That's all.'

'Ha, ha, ho, ho!' laughed all the little folk.
'What a joke! A whirlwind indeed! Whoever
heard of such an excuse! Ho ho!'

'Ho, ho, ho!' laughed Thimble, loudest of
all.

Brin-Brin tried to get loose but Thimble had
tied him up far too tightly. He was so angry
that his face was as red as a ripe tomato. How
dared Thimble play this trick on him! Just
wait! He would punish him when he got free!

But when would he get free? Nobody

offered to untie him. When night came and they were tired of laughing at him they all went home, except Thimble.

'They'll come back to laugh at you again tomorrow,' said Thimble. 'What a pity you have always been so proud and haughty, rude and selfish, Brin-Brin! If you hadn't been, you might have found someone kind enough to set you free.'

'Please set me free yourself,' said Brin-Brin, in a humble voice.

'What! Set you free to rush at me and hit me!' said Thimble. 'No, no, Brin-Brin – I'm not as foolish as that.'

Then Brin-Brin saw that things were really very serious. He might stay a prisoner for weeks. He must humble himself to the clever little pixie.

'Please, Thimble,' he begged. 'Set me free. I will promise not to hurt you. I have been a stupid, proud gnome, but I will never be again.'

'Will you pack your bags and go away if I set you free?' asked Thimble.

'Yes,' said Brin-Brin, at once, thinking that he certainly could never face seeing all the people of Go-and-See Village again. No – they would always laugh at him now. He must certainly go right away and never come back.

That was just what Thimble wanted! He at once ran to Brin-Brin and untied him. The gnome stretched his arms and legs and then set off in silence to his house. He packed up his bags and left his house that night, walking steadily towards the silver moon.

Thimble watched him go in delight. He had got rid of his unpleasant neighbour. Never again would he find his garden full of rubbish! Never again would he hear a voice singing loudly next door. Ho, ho, ho!

'Where has Brin-Brin gone?' asked the little folk next day.

'Oh, I untied him, told him to pack his bags and go,' said Thimble. 'So he's gone.'

'Dear, dear, what a wonder you are!' said the little folk, in delight. 'Let's hope he'll never come back!'

He never did – and I don't expect he ever will, do you?

A Shock For Freddie

There was once a little girl called Linda. She lived in a small cottage with her mother and father, and she was very fond of gardening. So her mother bought her a watering-can, a trowel, a fork, a broom and rake for her very own.

'You can keep them in the apple-shed,' said her mother, 'then they won't get mixed up with Daddy's things. There is plenty of room behind the apple-racks.'

So Linda kept her tools there. She was a

very good worker, and she always kept her tools clean and tidy. She never put any of them away dirty, and she used to rub the trowel and fork till they shone before she put them away.

They often used to talk about Linda, in the middle of the night, when they were all alone in the sweet-smelling apple-shed.

'She's a very nice child to belong to,' said the broom in its funny sweeping voice.

'She looks after us so well,' said the trowel, in its scrapy voice.

'Not like the boy next door,' said the watering-can. 'He simply throws his tools into the shed all dirty, and never cleans them at all. They are rusty, and three of them are broken.'

'His watering-can has a hole in the bottom,' said the rake.

'How dreadful!' said Linda's can, shivering on its shelf.

'His fork is broken,' said the broom.

'Dear, dear, what a horrid boy!' said Linda's fork. 'I *am* glad we don't belong to him! I hope he never comes here.'

Well, one day the boy next door *did* come to Linda's garden. His name was Freddie, and he was a fat, lazy boy, clumsy and careless. On the other side of the fence there was a little shed just like Linda's apple-shed, and one day when Freddie was peeping through the cracks in the side of it, he found that he could see right into the apple-shed next door.

And his greedy little eyes saw the red apples stored so carefully in the apple-racks there! Goodness me, how his mouth watered when he saw them!

'I shall wait until Linda and everyone next door are out,' said Freddie to himself, 'and then I shall climb over the fence, squeeze in at the shed window and eat a few apples. Nobody will know, and I shall have a fine feast.'

Well, that is exactly what he *did* do! The very next day he watched Linda and her father and mother go out to tea, and as soon as they were gone he climbed quickly over the fence and ran to the apple-shed. The door was locked, as he had thought it would be, but it didn't take him a minute to open the little window and squeeze himself through it.

Then what a fine time he had! He ate four of the biggest, reddest apples, and then climbed out of the window again, with two apples safely in his pocket.

The tools on the shelf behind the apples looked at one another in anger. How dare that horrid boy come into their shed and steal their apples?

'Linda will be blamed for taking them,' said the fork in a rage. 'She is the only person who comes here besides her mother and father.'

The fork was right. Linda *was* blamed for taking the apples, and she was very sad about it.

'But, Mummy, I didn't *touch* the apples,' she said. 'Truly I didn't. I would never take anything you told me not to, really I wouldn't.'

'Well, who *did* take them then?' said her mother. 'The door is always locked.'

The next week Freddie took some more apples, and Linda was scolded again. She cried bitterly and was very unhappy. The tools longed to tell her who the thief was, but they couldn't talk as she did. It was dreadful.

Then the broom had a wonderful idea.

'Let's punish Freddie and give him such a fright that he will never come to our shed again!' it said. 'I will sweep him off his feet, and you, watering-can, can water him from head to foot.'

'And I will rake him up and down,' said the rake.

'And we will dig under his toes and make holes for him to fall into,' said the fork and trowel in excitement. 'He deserves to be punished. Watering-can, it's pouring with rain now, so if you stick yourself out of the window, you will get full of raindrops – then you will be ready for Freddie!'

'Ready for Freddie!' sang all the tools, in glee.

Now it so happened that night that Freddie was sent to bed without any supper because he had been naughty. So he was very hungry indeed. He hadn't been in bed very long before he made up his mind to steal downstairs,

climb over the garden-wall, and go to the apple-shed next door. Then he would eat plenty of those lovely red apples there!

So off he went, and it wasn't long before he was in the shed. The tools felt most excited. Now they could do all they had planned to do!

Freddie felt about for the apple-racks. Then he quickly took four apples and stuffed them into a bag he had brought with him – and just as he did that, the watering-can carefully tipped itself up and began to water him!

'Ooh!' shouted Freddie in a fright, as the cold water soaked him from head to foot. 'What is it? Ooh! Stop!'

But the watering-can didn't stop until it had emptied all its water on to the frightened little thief. Then it was the rake's turn! It jumped up to Freddie and began to rake him up and down, tearing big holes in his sleeping-suit. Freddie tried to run away from it, but the fork and trowel hopped about in front of him, digging little holes under his toes.

'There are rats round my feet!' cried Freddie. 'Help! Help!'

Then the broom thought it would join in, and it began to sweep Freddie up as if he were dead leaves. Swish! Swish! Freddie called for help even more loudly, and this time Linda's father and mother heard him and came rushing out to the apple-shed to see what was the matter.

When they saw Freddie with the bag of apples in his hand they knew at once who had been the apple-thief. They took Freddie into their cottage and looked at him. He was wet, dirty and torn, and he cried with fright.

'What *have* you been doing in that shed?' asked Linda, peeping down the stairs in surprise.

'S-s-something w-w-watered me!' sobbed Freddie.

'My watering-can!' cried Linda.

'And then something raked me up and down!' wept Freddie.

'My garden rake!' said Linda.

'And rats kept digging holes under my feet, and then something swept me up!' sobbed the frightened boy.

'My fork and trowel and my broom!' cried Linda. 'They must have seen you stealing our apples and felt cross with you. Well, it serves you right.'

'Don't punish me for taking your apples,' begged Freddie, turning to Linda's father and mother.

'You have been well punished already,' said Linda's mother. 'Go back now to your own house. I am afraid that when your mother sees your torn sleeping-suit she will be very cross with you.'

So she was! Poor Freddie was well spanked and as he lay in bed again that night, he said to himself: 'Well, that's the last time I ever take anything that doesn't belong to me! I wonder what it was that treated me like that in the apple-shed. It couldn't *really* have been Linda's tools.'

But it was! Linda knew it and she thanked them very much next time she used them – and how she cleans and polishes them! They really are a wonderful sight to see.

THE ENID BLYTON TRUST FOR CHILDREN

We hope you have enjoyed the adventures of the children in this book. Please think for a moment about those children who are too ill to do the exciting things you and your friends do.

Help them by sending a donation, large or small, to the ENID BLYTON TRUST FOR CHILDREN. The trust will use all your gifts to help children who are sick or handicapped and need to be made happy and comfortable.

Please send your postal orders or cheques to:

The Enid Blyton Trust For Children,
International House
1 St Katharine's Way
London E1 9UN

Thank you very much for your help.